Watch your tail so that it doesn't get burnt.

Always use oven gloves when handling hot things.

Don't put your nose straight into the bowl to taste - use a clean spoon.

Don't forget the washing-up.

MUMMY BEAR'S

SANDWICHES

YOU WILL NEED:
bread,
chopping board,
butter,
filling of
your choice,
sharp knife
(to be used by
a grown-up).

1. Butter the bread evenly.

2. Add the filling.

HERE ARE SOME IDEAS

Cheese and tomato

Cucumber mayonnaise and watercress

Peanut butter and jam

Banana and honey

Tomato and basil leaves

3. Cut into quarters.

4. You can use cutters to make sandwich shapes.

5. Arrange on a plate. Serve with crisps

P|FEA

WS 2183374 5

D1578377

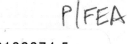

Mr Wolf can be contacted at
www.hungry-wolf.com

For Ramona and Lisa

First published in 2001 by Egmont Children's Books Limited,
a division of Egmont Holding Limited,
239 Kensington High Street, London W8 6SA
Text and illustrations copyright © Jan Fearnley 2001
Jan Fearnley has asserted her moral rights
A CIP catalogue record for this title is available from the British Library
Printed in Hong Kong
ISBN 0 416 19928 3
10 9 8 7 6 5 4 3 2 1

Mr Wolf
and the
Three Bears
Jan Fearnley

EGMONT CHILDREN'S BOOKS

It was a special day for Mr Wolf. He was
feeling very excited, because today his friends
the Three Bears were coming round for tea.
It was Baby Bear's birthday, and Mr Wolf was
planning a lovely party for everyone.

Mr Wolf wanted to cook a special dish for each one of his guests, and because there was such a lot to do, Grandma came along to help.

"We must be tidy and safe in the kitchen when we're cooking," reminded Grandma. "Let's wash our paws before we start, and then we can have some fun."

For Baby Bear's dish, they looked in the big recipe book. Soon they found the perfect thing to make.

A birthday cake!

Next they thought about Mummy Bear.
"I know she likes sandwiches," said Mr Wolf.
Grandma remembered there was a recipe in
her magazine.

They followed it carefully and soon there
was a big heap of sandwiches on the table,
all ready for the party.

Now it was time to make something for Daddy Bear. Grandma's favourite TV programme gave them lots of ideas.

"Those Huff Puff cakes sound good," said Mr Wolf.

"Good thinking," said Grandma. "We'd better make lots because he's a big bear."

They were easy to do.

Then it was Grandma's turn to pick something tasty.
But she couldn't decide what she wanted.

Mr Wolf had a brainwave.

Mr Wolf helped Grandma look on the internet for some ideas. At <u>www.hungry-wolf.com</u> Grandma found a recipe she fancied – Cheesy Snipsnaps!

They printed out the recipe and set to work.

Mr Wolf and Grandma still had a lot to do before their guests arrived.

They blew up balloons,

wrapped Baby Bear's present,

laid the table

and made some party hats.

Grandma arranged some flowers.

Then they tidied the house from top . . .

to bottom . . .

until it looked lovely.

"Ready!" said Mr Wolf, just as
they heard a knock on the door.

"Come in! Welcome!" cried Mr Wolf.
"Happy Birthday, Baby Bear!"

But somebody came barging in before them!

IT WAS GOLDILOCKS!

"Let me come in, Mr Wolf," she demanded.
"I smell nice things a-cooking."
"What have you brought her for?" whispered
Mr Wolf. "She always causes trouble."

"She followed us through the woods," said Daddy Bear. "There was nothing we could do! She said she was invited too."

"What a fibber!" said Mr Wolf.

"Don't be mean! Let the child come in," called Grandma from her chair. "But you'd better behave yourself, Goldilocks," she warned.

"Yeah, yeah," shrugged Goldilocks, tossing her curls. "I promise."

But it wasn't long before Goldilocks forgot her promise.

When they were dancing, she trod on Mr Wolf's toe and didn't say sorry.

When they played pass the parcel, Goldilocks took off all the wrappers instead of just one.

When they played musical chairs, Goldilocks was too
rough – and she cheated!

Grandma didn't join in the games. She just sat in
her chair, as grandmas often do, watching. "I think it's
time for tea," she said. But . . .

. . . someone had got there first!

"Somebody's had a bite out of this cake," said Daddy Bear.

"Somebody's been at this sandwich, too," said Mummy Bear.

"Mine's nearly all gone!" cried Baby Bear. "This always happens to me!"

"Your food's yukky," complained Goldilocks, with her
cheeks bulging. Her table manners were atrocious!
Poor Mr Wolf. "My party is a disaster!" he whimpered.
Grandma smiled at Mr Wolf and slowly got to her feet.
"It's time for another game," she said.

"Let's play hide and seek."
"Boring," said Goldilocks.
"I always win."
"We'll see," said Grandma.

Everyone ran off to hide.
Grandma counted to one
hundred. "Coming! Ready
or not!" she called.

She took a while . . .

. . . but she did find
everybody eventually . . .

. . . that is, all except
for Goldilocks.
She was nowhere to be seen.

"What a rude girl," said Mummy Bear. "She nearly
ruined our party and now she's gone off without
saying thank you."

"Never mind," said Grandma. "I've got a surprise."
She disappeared into the kitchen . . .

. . . and emerged with a beautiful great big pie,
all steaming hot from the oven, with a golden,
melt-in-the-mouth crumbly pastry crust.

"Clever Grandma!" everybody cheered.

"Let's gobble it up while it's hot!" said Mr Wolf.
"Not just yet," said Grandma. "I think this is a
dish best served cold."

And as they waited for the golden pie to cool, Grandma giggled to herself and settled back to enjoy the rest of the party.

"Save me a big piece," she said, ". . . a very big piece. I'm starving!"

DADDY BEAR'S HUFF PUFFS

YOU WILL NEED:

175g chocolate, 50g butter,
2 tablespoons syrup,
125g rice crispies, cornflakes or huff puffs,
paper cake cases.

1. Put butter and syrup into pan.

2. Add the chocolate. Save some for the pan please, Grandma.

3. Heat gently until melted.

4. Add the crispies and mix together.

5. Carefully spoon into cases. Allow to cool, then put in the fridge to harden.

Don't balance them on your nose. It's not polite!

...GH... SNIPSNA...

YOU WILL NEED:

125g self raising flour, pinch salt, 1/2 teaspoon ᴏf mustard powder, 50g butteᵣ 75g grated cheese, 1 egg.

1. Sieve the flour, salt and mustard into a bowl.

3. Roll out dough on a floured surface until quite thin. Use cutters or a knife to make shapes.

5. Cool on a wire rack. They taste great on the day but will also keep in a tin for a few days.